AESOP'S
FABLES

AESOP'S FABLES

ILLUSTRATED BY
Charles Santore

JellyBean Press
NEW YORK

Copyright © 1988 by dilithium Press, Ltd., JellyBean Press Division.
Color illustrations copyright © 1988 by Charles Santore.
All rights reserved.

This 1988 edition is published by JellyBean Press, a division of dilithium Press, Ltd.,
distributed by Crown Publishers, Inc., 225 Park Avenue South, New York, New York 10003.

DILITHIUM is a registered trademark and JELLYBEAN PRESS is a trademark
of dilithium Press, Ltd.

Printed and bound in Italy

Book design by Madge Schultz

Library of Congress Cataloging-in-Publication Data

Aesop's fables. English. Selections. 1988.
    Aesop's fables/illustrated by Charles Santore.—1988 ed.
        p.   cm.
    Summary: an illustrated collection of twenty-four Aesop fables selected from
those populated only by animals, arranged in categories such as lion fables, fox fables,
and wolf fables.
    1. Fables. [1. Fables. 2. Animals—Folklore.] I. Santore, Charles, ill.
II. Title.
PZ8.2.A254   1988b
398.2'452—dc19
[E]   88-15910
ISBN 0-517-64115-1   CIP
                                                                        AC

h g f e d c

This book is for my mother, Nellie Santore,
in gratitude for passing on to me a precious gift—
the ability to draw.

CHARLES SANTORE

NOTE ON THE TEXT

The text for this edition of *Aesop's Fables* has been chosen in close collaboration with Charles Santore, the illustrator of this collection, from an excellent classic translation, notable for its precise and direct language and strong visual images. The modern reader should enjoy the occasional quaintness of its traditional style, and also rejoice in its elegance, flavor, and wit.

CLAIRE BOOSS
Editor

CONTENTS

FOREWORD

Aesop. The name is as familiar to most of us as Santa Claus. From earliest nursery school or kindergarten days almost every child is treated to "story time," and the best stories for little people have always included the fables of Aesop. We can remember "The Fox and the Grapes," "The Hare and the Tortoise," "The Lion and the Mouse," and most certainly we can remember the moral to be learned from those we can recall. Yet Aesop himself remains a name that most adults remember with some confusion. And rightfully so. For Aesop was, as far as the best researchers can conclude, a collective name, a device for bringing the best and earliest fables together in one volume. In this new edition, the distinguished and prize-winning illustrator Charles Santore has reinterpreted twenty-four of his favorites of these classic tales in stunning color portrayals with great authenticity and feeling.

The artist states, "Deciding which animal fables to include was based on my own visual preference for one fable over another. A further consideration was drawing and painting an interesting variety of creatures. Many of

the best-loved, most well-known fables are included in
this volume and some not so well-known. All are
particular favorites of mine." The enthusiasm of the
artist for his subject matter has provided us with both a
visual banquet and a unique organization of the fables as
conceived by Mr. Santore.

As Aesop, the name, has come to represent all of the
original creators of these tales from earliest times, so,
Mr. Santore declares, do all the animals represent a
specific character trait and a specific "pecking order." In
his research for the project, Santore read an introduction
to an early twentieth century volume of *Aesop's Fables*
written by G. K. Chesterton and found it a revelation
which deepened his understanding of fables in general
and in particular influenced his choice of those included
in this collection and his pictorial approach to them.

"The moment I read Chesterton's explanation," says

Santore, "I could visualize the majestic lion always occupying center stage; the fox forever sidling up to a situation, never confronting it directly; the sheep always doomed, plodding on, never-comprehending pawns in the game of life. 'They have no choice, they cannot be anything but themselves,' is the way Chesterton states it. Each animal—the wolf, the clever fox, the silly crow—represents and symbolizes some particular aspect of the human condition. Whatever the situation, the animal's reaction is always predictable. This is true of all the creatures that populate the fables, and they never disappoint us. They are never more or less. That is the great lesson and the essence of the fable."

Based on this exciting revelation, Santore has grouped the fables by species: lion fables, fox fables, wolf fables, and so on, together in a continuum. Arranged in this way, the reader (and the child-listener) can follow each creature from one situation to another and can better gain an understanding of the particular animal's role as a parody of human behavior. The illustrations further enhance and empower this point. As we follow the lion from story to story and from illustration to illustration, the artist's brilliant technique of personification of the beast as king grows and takes hold in our minds. The little child has each fable reinforced by the subsequent one, and Santore's art provides a strong supportive form for the moral each fable is depicting.

Santore has further sharpened his intent by including only those fables populated by animals. Again, he follows Chesterton's dictum that "there can be no good fable with human beings in it. There can be no good fairy tale without them." Santore states, "I saw immediately the implications of his statement. Fables that substitute animals exclusively in place of people avoid the distracting problems of gender, nationality, race, time, and social strata. The animal fables above all the rest apply to us all. They are truly timeless and universal lessons."

In his own way, Santore is discovering what all children intuitively know: a puppy or a kitten is to be loved and is infinitely loving; a rat is to be hated; a frog is grotesque. Stuffed animals are more popular with young children than dolls, for animals' expressions, even in mass-produced plush form, are more expressive and appealing than a doll's expression. Santore's animals are not teddy bears by any means—the wolves are masterfully evil, the lambs unstable even in stance, the lions wildly macho. But the real story lies in the eyes of each creature he has created: fear, arrogance, indifference, craftiness, stupidity, and a bushel of other traits leap out from the vibrant pictures and reach into the innermost well of understanding of any viewer.

At last, we have an edition of Aesop as symbolic and

astute in organization and visual representation as the versions that the various "Aesop"s created. Santore remarks, "Making the pictures to illustrate these wonderful stories was both an exciting and, at the same time, a humbling experience for me. I am grateful for such a rich and rewarding opportunity." And we, the recipients of Mr. Santore's understanding and artistry, are doubly grateful. His excitement is contagious, his humility a further example of the generosity and selflessness that shine through every page of this magnificent edition.

PATRICIA BARRETT PERKINS

Baltimore, Maryland
1988

ACKNOWLEDGMENTS

I am grateful to Caryn Malitzky, the associate publisher, and Don Bender, the art director, for suggesting that I add my vision to a collection of the fables; to Claire Booss, the editor, for her invaluable assistance and sensitive, careful research on this project; and to Madge Schultz, the designer, for her graceful, elegant design for this book. Thanks are also due to Laura Torrecilla, Senior Production Manager, and Susan Wein, Production Supervisor, for the creative, exacting, and conscientious production skill that went into achieving the finished book.

C.S.

AESOP'S FABLES

The WOLF
and the
CRANE

A WOLF once got a bone stuck in his throat: so he went to a Crane and begged her to put her long bill down his throat and pull it out. "I'll make it worth your while," he added. The Crane did as she was asked and got the bone out quite easily. The Wolf thanked her warmly and was just turning away, when she cried, "What about that fee of mine?" "Well, what about it?" snapped the Wolf, baring his teeth as he spoke. "You can go about boasting that you once put your head into a Wolf's mouth and didn't get it bitten off. What more do you want?"

The WOLF
a n d   t h e
LAMB

A WOLF came upon a Lamb straying from the flock and felt some reluctance about taking the life of so helpless a creature without some plausible excuse: so he cast about for a grievance and said at last, "Last year, sir, you grossly insulted me." "That is impossible, sir," bleated the Lamb, "for I wasn't born then." "Well," retorted the Wolf, "you feed in my pastures." "That cannot be," replied the Lamb, "for I have never yet tasted grass." "You drink from my spring, then," continued the Wolf. "Indeed, sir," said the poor Lamb, "I have never yet drunk anything but my mother's milk." "Well, anyhow," said the Wolf, "I'm not going without my dinner," and he sprang upon the Lamb and devoured it without more ado.

The WOLF in SHEEP'S CLOTHING

A WOLF resolved to disguise himself in order that he might prey upon a flock of sheep without fear of detection: so he clothed himself in a sheepskin and slipped among the sheep when they were out at pasture. He completely deceived the shepherd, and when the flock was penned for the night, he was shut in with them. But that very night as it happened, the shepherd, requiring a supply of mutton for the table, laid his hands on the Wolf, mistaking him for a Sheep, and finished him off with his knife on the spot.

The VAIN JACKDAW

JUPITER, KING OF THE GODS, announced that he intended to appoint a King over the birds, and he named a day on which they were to appear before his throne when he would select the most beautiful of them all to be their ruler. Wishing to look their best on the occasion, they retired to the banks on a stream, where they busied themselves in washing and preening their feathers. The Jackdaw was there along with the rest and realized that, with his ugly plumage, he would have no chance of being chosen as he was: so he waited till they were all gone, and then picked up the most gaudy of the feathers they had dropped and fastened them about his own body, with the result that he looked gayer than any of them. When the appointed day came, the birds assembled before Jupiter's throne; and after passing them in review, he was about to make the Jackdaw King, when all the rest set upon the King-elect, stripped him of his borrowed plumes, and exposed him for the Jackdaw that he was.

The LION and the WILD ASS

A LION and a Wild Ass went out hunting together: the latter was to run down the prey by his superior speed, and the former would then come up and dispatch it. They met with great success; and when it came to sharing the spoil,

the Lion divided it all into three equal portions. "I will take the first," said he, "because I am King of the Beasts; I will also take the second, because, as your partner, I am entitled to half of what remains; and as for the third—well, unless you give it up to me and take off pretty quickly, the third, believe me, will make you feel very sorry for yourself!"

The LION and the MOUSE

A LION asleep in his lair was awakened by a Mouse running over his face. Losing his temper, he seized it with his paw and was about to kill it. The Mouse, terrified, piteously entreated him to spare its life. "Please let me go," it cried, "and one day I will repay you for your kindness." The idea of so insignificant a creature ever being able to do anything for him amused the Lion so much that he laughed aloud and good-humoredly let it go. But the Mouse's chance came, after all.

One day the Lion got entangled in a net which had been spread for game by some hunters, and the Mouse heard and recognized his roars of anger and ran to the spot. Without more ado, it set to work to gnaw the ropes with its teeth and succeeded before long in setting the Lion free. "There!" said the Mouse. "You laughed at me when I promised I would repay you: but now you see, even a Mouse can help a Lion."

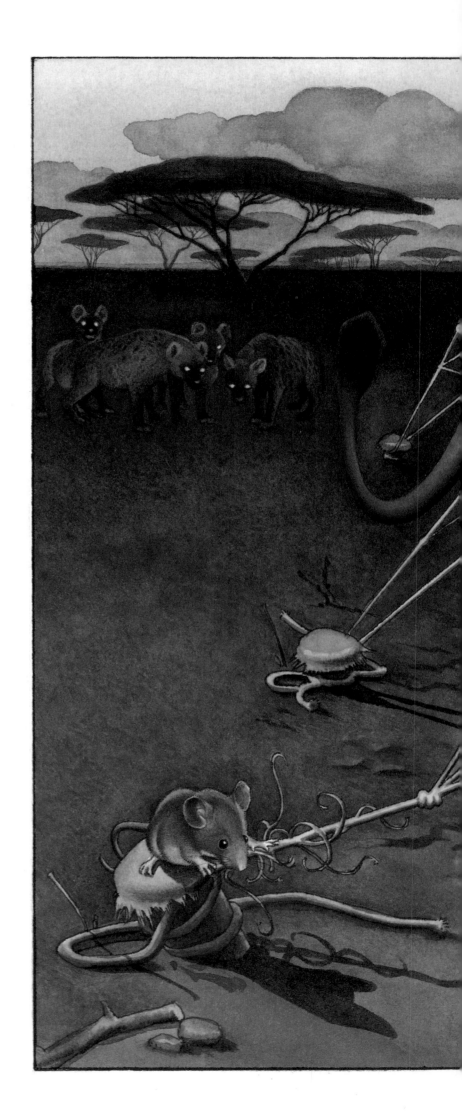

The ASS
in the
LION'S SKIN

AN Ass found a Lion's skin and dressed himself up in it. Then he went about frightening every one he met, for they all took him to be a Lion, men and beasts alike, and took to their heels when they saw him coming. Elated by the success of his trick, he loudly brayed in triumph. The Fox heard him and recognized him at once for the Ass he was and said to him, "Oho, my friend, it's you, is it? I, too, should have been afraid if I hadn't heard your voice."

The OLD LION and the FOX

A LION, enfeebled by age and no longer able to procure food for himself by force, determined to do so by cunning. Taking himself to a cave, he lay down inside and pretended to be sick; and whenever any of the other animals entered to

inquire after his health, he sprang upon them and devoured them. Many lost their lives in this way, till one day a Fox called at the cave and, having a suspicion of the truth, addressed the Lion from outside instead of going in and asked him how he was. He replied that he was in a very bad way: "But," said he, "why do you stand outside? Pray come in." "I should have done so," answered the Fox, "if I hadn't noticed that all the footprints point toward the cave and none the other way."

The MONKEY a s KING

A T A GATHERING of all the animals the Monkey danced and delighted them so much that they made him their King. The Fox, however, was very much disgusted at the promotion of the Monkey: so having one day found a trap with a piece of meat in it, he took the Monkey there and said to him, "Here is a dainty morsel I have found, sire; I did not take it myself, because I thought it ought to be reserved for you, our King. Will you be pleased to accept it?" The Monkey went at once for the meat and got caught in the trap. Then he bitterly reproached the Fox for leading him into danger; but the Fox only laughed and said, "O Monkey, you call yourself King of the Beasts and haven't more sense than to be taken in like that!"

The FOX
and the
GRAPES

A HUNGRY FOX saw some fine bunches of Grapes hanging from a vine that was trained along a high tree and did his best to reach them by jumping as high as he could into the air. But it was all in vain, for they were just out of reach: so he gave up trying and walked away with an air of dignity and unconcern, remarking, "I thought those Grapes were ripe, but I see now they are quite sour."

The WILD BOAR
and the
FOX

A WILD BOAR was engaged in sharpening his tusks upon the trunk of a tree in the forest when a Fox came by and, seeing what he was at, said to him, "Why are you doing that, pray? The huntsmen are not out today, and there are no other dangers at hand that I can see." "True, my friend," replied the Boar, "but the instant my life is in danger I shall need to use my tusks. There'll be no time to sharpen them then."

The FOX
and the
CROW

A CROW was sitting on a branch of a tree with a piece of cheese in her beak when a Fox observed her and set his wits to work to discover some way of getting the cheese. Coming and standing under the tree he looked up and said, "What a noble bird I see above me! Her beauty is without equal, the hue of her plumage exquisite. If only her voice is as sweet as her looks are fair, she ought without doubt to be Queen of the Birds." The Crow was hugely flattered by this, and just to show the Fox that she could sing, she gave a loud caw. Down came the cheese, of course, and the Fox, snatching it up, said, "You have a voice, madam, I see: what you want is wits."

The CROW
and the
SWAN

A CROW was filled with envy on seeing the beautiful white plumage of a Swan and thought it was due to the water in which the Swan constantly bathed and swam. So he left the neighborhood of the inns, where he got his living by taking bits of meat left from the plates of the diners, and went and lived among the pools and streams. But though he bathed and washed his feathers many times a day, he didn't make them any whiter and at last died of hunger into the bargain.

You may change your habits but not your nature.

The EAGLE
and the
CROW

ONE DAY A CROW saw an Eagle swoop down on a Lamb and carry it aloft in its talons. "My word," said the Crow, "I'll do that myself." So it flew high up into the air and then came shooting down with a great whirring of wings on to the back of a big Ram, with the intention of carrying it off. It had no sooner alighted, than its claws got caught fast in the wool, and nothing it could do was of any use: there it stuck, flapping away and only making things worse instead of better. By and by up came the Shepherd. "Oho," he said, "so that's what you'd be doing, is it?" And he took the Crow and clipped its wings and carried it home to his children. It looked so odd that they didn't know what to make of it. "What sort of bird is it, Father?" they asked. "It's a Crow," he replied, "and nothing but a Crow: but it wants to be taken for an Eagle."

The TWO GOATS

TWO PROUD GOATS happened to meet on the opposite cliffs of a high mountain range where a fierce river ran below through a rocky valley. The only bridge across the chasm was a fallen tree so narrow as to frighten two mice passing each other at the same time. Both stubborn Goats felt that they had the right to cross the river first; so setting one hoof at a time upon the slender log, they found themselves head to head in the middle of the bridge. Neither Goat would give way to the other, and finally they both fell headlong into the roaring waters below.

The TORTOISE
and the
EAGLE

A TORTOISE, discontented with his lowly life and envious of the birds he saw enjoying themselves in the air, begged an Eagle to teach him to fly. The Eagle protested that it was idle for him to try, as nature had not provided him with wings; but the Tortoise pressed him with entreaties and promises of treasure, insisting that it could only be a question of learning the craft of the air: so at length the Eagle consented to do the best he could for him and picked him up in his talons. Soaring with him to a great height in the sky he then let him go, and the wretched Tortoise fell headlong into the sea.

The OX
a n d t h e
FROG

T WO LITTLE FROGS were playing about at the edge
of a pool when an Ox came down to the water to
drink and by accident trod on one of them and crushed
him. When the old Frog missed him, she asked his
brother where he was. "He is dead, Mother," said the
little Frog; "an enormous big creature with four legs
came to our pool this morning and trampled him down
in the mud." "Enormous, was he? Was he as big as this?"
said the Frog, puffing herself out to look as big as
possible. "Oh! yes, *much* bigger," was the answer. The
Frog puffed herself out still more. "Was he as big as
this?" said she. "Oh! yes, yes, Mother, MUCH bigger,"
said the little Frog. And yet again she puffed and puffed
herself out till she was almost as round as a ball. "Cease,
Mother, to puff yourself out," said the little Frog, "and do
not be angry; for you would sooner burst then
successfully imitate the hugeness of that creature."

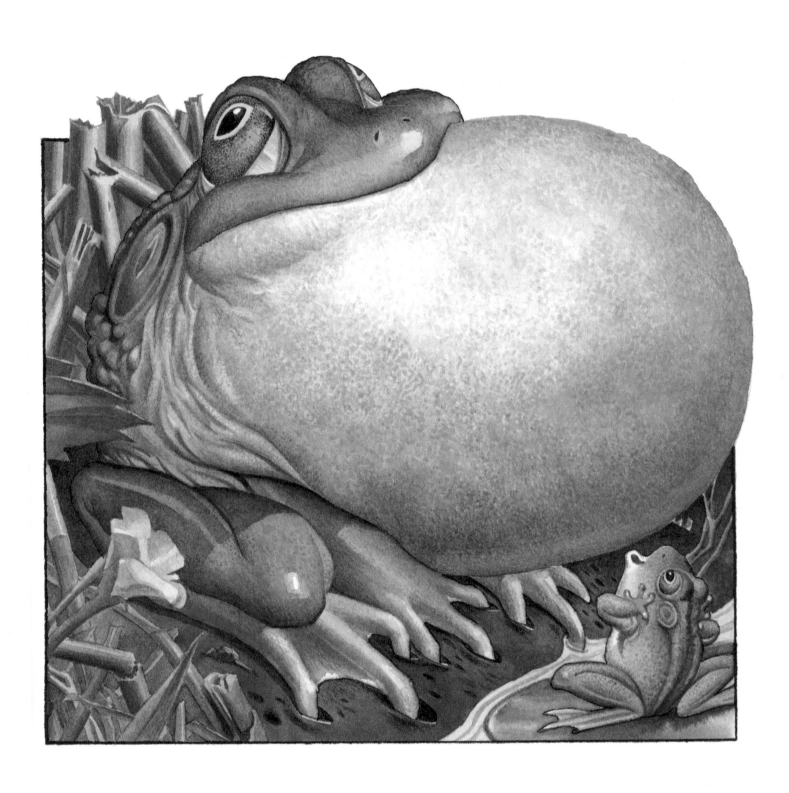

The CRAB
a n d
HIS MOTHER

AN OLD CRAB said to her son, "Why do you walk sideways like that, my son? You ought to walk straight." The Young Crab replied, "Show me how, dear Mother, and I'll follow your example." The Old Crab tried but tried in vain, and then saw how foolish she had been to find fault with her child.

The HERON

A HERON went wading one early morning to take his breakfast from the shallows of a stream. There were many Fish in the water, but the stately Heron thought he could find better. "Such small fry is certainly not suitable fare for a Heron," he remarked to himself. And as a choice young Perch swam by, the Heron tipped his long bill in the air and snapped, "No, sir, I certainly wouldn't open my beak for that!" The sun grew higher and all the Fish left the shallows for the cool, deep, middle of the stream. When the Heron could find no trace of a Fish left in the stream, he was very grateful to finally break his fast on a mere snail.

The TOWN MOUSE and

A TOWN MOUSE and a Country Mouse were acquaintances, and the Country Mouse one day invited his friend to come and see him at his home in the fields. The Town Mouse came, and they sat down to a dinner of barleycorns and roots, the latter of which had a distinctly earthy flavor. The fare was not much to the taste of the guest, and presently he broke out with, "My poor dear friend, you live here no better than the ants. Now, you should just see how I fare! My larder is a regular horn of plenty. You must come and stay with me, and I promise you, you shall live on the fat of the land." So when he returned to town he took the Country Mouse with him and showed him a larder containing

the COUNTRY MOUSE

flour and oatmeal and figs and honey and dates. The Country Mouse had never seen anything like it and sat down to enjoy the luxuries his friend provided; but before they had begun, the door of the larder opened and someone came in. The two Mice scampered off and hid themselves in a narrow and exceedingly uncomfortable hole. Presently, when all was quiet, they ventured out again; but someone else came in, and off they scuttled again. This was too much for the visitor. "Good-bye," said he, "I'm off. You live in the lap of luxury, I can see, but you are surrounded by dangers; whereas at home I can enjoy my simple dinner of roots and corn in peace."

The BEAR and the BEES

A BEAR was once searching for berries in the woods when he came across an old log where Bees had stored their honey. Wishing to find out whether the Bees were at home, he sniffed around the log with some caution. Along came a Bee on his way home from the fields with more honey, and on seeing the Bear, he angrily leapt upon his nose, stung him once, and flew swiftly into his house. The wretched Bear then rushed at the log with his teeth and claws, but the entire nest of Bees poured out and swarmed all over his body. Stumbling away in agony, the Bear was only able to save himself by falling headfirst into a nearby pond.

The GRASSHOPPER
and the
ANTS

ONE FINE DAY in winter some Ants were busy drying their store of corn, which had got rather damp during a long spell of rain. Presently, up came a Grasshopper and begged them to spare her a few grains, "For," she said, "I'm simply starving." The Ants stopped work for a moment, though this was against their principles. "May we ask," said they, "what you were doing with yourself all last summer? Why didn't you collect a store of food for the winter?" "The fact is," replied the Grasshopper, "I was so busy singing that I hadn't the time." "If you spent the summer singing," replied the Ants, "you can't do better than spend the winter dancing." And they chuckled and went on with their work.

The GRASSHOPPER
and the
OWL

A N OWL, who lived in a hollow tree, was in the habit of feeding by night and sleeping by day; but her slumbers were greatly disturbed by the chirping of a Grasshopper, who had taken up his abode in the branches. She begged him repeatedly to have some consideration for her comfort, but the Grasshopper, if anything, only chirped the louder. At last the Owl could stand it no longer and was determined to rid herself of the pest by means of a trick. Addressing herself to the Grasshopper, she said in her most pleasant manner, "As I cannot sleep for your song, which, believe me, is as sweet as the sound of a harp, I have a mind to taste some nectar, which I was given the other day. Won't you come in and join me?" The Grasshopper was flattered by the praise of his song, and his mouth, too, watered at the mention of the delicious drink, so he said he would be delighted. No sooner had he gotten inside the hollow where the Owl was sitting than she pounced upon him and ate him up.

The HARE
a n d t h e
TORTOISE

ONE DAY a Hare was making fun of a Tortoise for being so slow upon his feet. "Wait a bit," said the Tortoise, "I'll run a race with you, and I'll wager that I win." "Oh, well," replied the Hare, who was much amused at the idea, "let's try and see;" and it was soon agreed that the Fox should set a course for them and be the judge. When the time came both started off together, but the Hare was soon so far ahead that he thought he might as well have a rest: so down he lay and fell fast asleep. Meanwhile the Tortoise kept plodding on and in time reached the goal. At last the Hare woke up with a start and dashed on at his fastest pace, but only to find that the Tortoise had already won the race.

Slow and steady wins the race.